MR. HAPPY

by Roger Hargreaves

On the other side of the world, where the sun shines hotter than here, and where the trees are a hundred feet tall, there is a country called Happyland.

As you might very well expect everybody who lives in Happyland is as happy as the day is long. Wherever you go you see smiling faces all round. It's such a happy place that even the flowers seem to smile in Happyland.

And, as well as all the people being happy, all the animals in Happyland are happy as well.

If you've never seen a mouse smile, or a cat, or a dog, or even a worm – go to Happyland!

This is a story about someone who lived there who happened to be called Mr Happy.

Mr Happy was fat and round, and happy!

He lived in a small cottage beside a lake at the foot of a mountain and close to a wood in Happyland.

One day, while Mr Happy was out walking through the tall trees in those woods near his home, he came across something which was really rather extraordinary.

There in the trunk of one of the very tall trees was a door.

Not a very large door, but nevertheless a door. Certainly a door. A small, narrow, yellow door.

Definitely a door!

"I wonder who lives here?" thought Mr Happy to himself, and he turned the handle of that small, narrow, yellow door.

The door wasn't locked and it swung open quite easily.

Just inside the small, narrow, yellow door was a small, narrow, winding staircase, leading downwards.

Mr Happy squeezed his rather large body through the rather thin doorway and began to walk down the stairs.

The stairs went round and round and down and down and round and down and down and round.

Eventually, after a long time, Mr Happy reached the bottom of the staircase.

He looked around and saw, there in front of him, another small, narrow door. But this one was red.

Mr Happy knocked at the door.

"Who's there?" said a voice. A sad, squeaky sort of voice. "Who's there?"

Mr Happy pushed open the red door slowly, and there, sitting on a stool, was somebody who looked exactly like Mr Happy, except that he didn't look happy at all.

In fact he looked downright miserable.

"Hello," said Mr Happy. "I'm Mr Happy."

"Oh, are you indeed," sniffed the person who looked like Mr Happy but wasn't. "Well, my name is Mr Miserable, and I'm the most miserable person in the world."

"Why are you so miserable?" asked Mr Happy.

"Because I am," replied Mr Miserable.

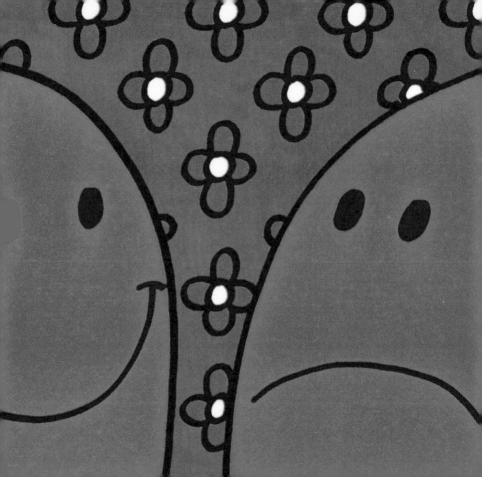

"How would you like to be happy like me?" asked Mr Happy.

"I'd give anything to be happy," said Mr Miserable. "But I'm so miserable I don't think I could ever be happy," he added miserably.

Mr Happy made up his mind quickly. "Follow me," he said.

"Where to?" asked Mr Miserable.

"Don't argue," said Mr Happy, and he went out through the small, narrow, red door.

Mr Miserable hesitated, and then followed.

Up and up the winding staircase they went. Up and up and round and round and up and round and round and up until they came out into the wood.

"Follow me," said Mr Happy again, and they both set off through the wood back to Mr Happy's cottage.

Mr Miserable stayed in Mr Happy's cottage for quite some time. And during that time the most remarkable thing happened.

Because he was living in Happyland Mr Miserable ever so slowly stopped being miserable and started to be happy.

His mouth stopped turning down at the corners.

And ever so slowly it started turning up at the corners.

And eventually Mr Miserable did something that he'd never done in the whole of his life.

He smiled!

And then he chuckled, which turned into a giggle, which became a laugh. A big booming hearty huge giant large enormous laugh.

And Mr Happy was so surprised that he started to laugh as well. And both of them laughed and laughed.

They laughed until their sides hurt and their eyes watered.

Mr Miserable and Mr Happy laughed and laughed and laughed and laughed.

They went outside and still they laughed.

And because they were laughing so much everybody who saw them started laughing as well. Even the birds in the trees started to laugh at the thought of somebody called Mr Miserable who just couldn't stop laughing.

And that's really the end of the story except to say that if you ever feel as miserable as Mr Miserable used to you know exactly what to do, don't you?

Just turn your mouth up at the corners.

Go on!

Fantastic offers for Mr. Men fans!

Collect all your Mr. Men or Little Miss books in these superb durable collectors' cases!
Only £5.99 inc. postage and packing, these wipe-clean, hard-wearing cases will give all your Mr. Men or Little Miss books a beautiful new home!

Keep track of your collection with this giant-sized double-sided Mr. Men and Little Miss Collectors' poster.
Collect 6 tokens and we will send you a brilliant giant-sized double-sided collectors' poster! Simply tape a £1 coin to cover postage and packaging in the space provided and fill out the form overleaf.

STICK £1 COIN HERE (for poster only)

Only need a few Mr. Men or Little Miss to complete your set? You can order any of the titles on the back of the books from our Mr. Men order line on 0870 787 1724. Orders should be delivered between 5 and 7 working days.

=== **TO BE COMPLETED BY AN ADULT** ===

To apply for any of these great offers, ask an adult to complete the details below and send this whole page with the appropriate payment and tokens, to: MR. MEN CLASSIC OFFER, PO BOX 715, HORSHAM RH12 5WG

☐ Please send me a giant-sized double-sided collectors' poster.

AND ☐ I enclose 6 tokens and have taped a £1 coin to the other side of this page.

☐ Please send me ☐ Mr. Men Library case(s) and/or ☐ Little Miss library case(s) at £5.99 each inc P&P

☐ I enclose a cheque/postal order payable to Egmont UK Limited for £.................

OR ☐ Please debit my MasterCard / Visa / Maestro / Delta account (delete as appropriate) for £.................

Card no. ☐☐☐☐ ☐☐☐☐ ☐☐☐☐ ☐☐☐☐ ☐☐☐☐   Security code ☐☐☐

Issue no. (if available) ☐   Start Date ☐☐/☐☐/☐☐   Expiry Date ☐☐/☐☐/☐☐

Fan's name: ....   Date of birth: ....

Address: ....

....

                                                                 Postcode: ....

Name of parent / guardian: ....

Email for parent / guardian: ....

Signature of parent / guardian: ....

Please allow 28 days for delivery. Offer is only available while stocks last. We reserve the right to change the terms of this offer at any time and we offer a 14 day money back guarantee. This does not affect your statutory rights. Offers apply to UK only.

☐ We may occasionally wish to send you information about other Egmont children's books.
If you would rather we didn't, please tick this box.

Ref: MRM 001